FRANKIE

CURVY GIRLS CAN BOOK TWO

SADIE KING

LET'S BE BESTIES!

A few times a month I send out an email with new releases, special deals and sneak peeks of what I'm working on. If you want to get on the list I'd love to meet you!

When you join you'll get access to all my bonus content which includes a couple of free short and steamy romances plus bonus scenes for selected books.

Sign up here:
authorsadieking.com/bonus-scenes

FRANKIE

CURVY GIRLS CAN

An enemies to lovers short and steamy romance.

Frankie

My mom's dying wish to reopen her beauty salon and make it the beating heart of Maple Springs again. So, when Mr. William Fletcher strides in with his big-city swagger, fat investment portfolio, and plans to bulldoze the salon along with the other shops for a soulless apartment complex, I'm livid.

Tradition and community are everything here, and William Fletcher knows nothing about either. Too bad my traitorous body didn't get the memo. Every time he's near, my heart races, my brain short-circuits, and my panties practically combust.

Can I save my salon and stick to my principles, or will I lose it all—including my heart—to the man I should hate?

Billy

I'm here to build, not make friends. This dying block of shops? Perfect for my next development.

The only snag? Frankie—fierce, fiery, and fiercely opposed to my plans. She's determined to stop me, and I'm determined not to let her. Except, every time we clash, I find myself distracted by her curves and captivated by her fire.

She says I don't care about her town. She's wrong. I do

care...just not enough to let her stop me. But every tussle with her only leaves me wanting more.

She might steal my focus—and maybe even my heart—but she won't stop my vision.

Frankie is book two in the *Curvy Girls Can* series—fast, fun, and steamy instalove stories about bold, beautiful women and the men who fall hard and fast for them.

1

FRANKIE

"Can you believe this?" I wave the planning notice at Janie as I stride toward the shop counter.

"What the fuck?" squawks Rufus, a bright blue Macaw, as he hops from one foot to the other on his wooden perch.

"Exactly." I nod to the parrot and he waggles his head up and down.

Bessie, a large black cat sprawled out on top of the shop counter, eyes me lazily as her tail swishes back and forth.

Janie looks up from the book she's reading and squints at the notice.

"Proposed residential apartment development," I read out the heading of the flyer.

Janie shrugs her shoulders and looks back down at her book. "Lots of development going on. Whereabouts is this one?"

Janie's a good friend, but her lack of interest in anything other than animals and books can be infuriating. "It's here. Right here."

She keeps reading. "In town?"

"Yes in town. Right here in town. On this exact spot." I spread my arms to indicate her pet shop and almost knock Rufus off his perch. The parrot squawks at me angrily. "Your shop, my salon, and all the other shops on this corner."

Janie looks up and frowns. "They can't build apartments if our shops are here."

"That's exactly what they're proposing."

Bessie jumps onto Janie's lap, and she strokes her distractedly. "But what about Pet Corner?"

"According to..." I glance at the professional-looking notice on crisp white paper and scan it for the company name, "Fletcher Associates, it's a 'disused part of the main street where shops are boarded up and customers no longer wish to frequent.'"

Janie looks indignant. "I have plenty of customers." She surveys the pet shop, empty but for the two of us and a bunch of animals. "It's not as busy at it used to be when Dad ran it. But some of my customers have been coming here for years to get their pet supplies."

I nod in agreement. The eccentric pet lady with the sweary parrot is well known in Maple Springs. "You're an institution in this town." I say carefully.

"What do Fletcher Associates have to say about that? Where are we supposed to go?"

I glance at the notice again. "There are premises on Burlap Street that would be suitable for any of the retail shops that wish to remain open."

She splutters. "Wish to remain open?"

I share her outrage. "No one goes down Burlap Street. The only places down there are a tattoo parlor and a florist. Hardly enough room for your menagerie. And what about my salon?"

Janie gives me a sympathetic look. "You have been closed for a while," she says tentatively.

"That's not the point." I fold my arms crossly. "You know I'm getting the salon ready to open again."

"I know that. But to this developer, it's just another boarded up shop that could be something else."

I squint at her. "Whose side are you on?"

"Yours of course, but I'm just saying. You can see how it must look."

She's right. The salon's been shut up ever since Mom got too sick to work. Since she passed away I've been working hard to get the money together to reopen, and I'm almost there. But it's been over a year since it closed its doors.

I sigh heavily and Rufus mutters something that sounds like. "Asshole." Which sums up my opinion of this developer.

"I'm not going to let them turn Mom's salon into someone's tiny apartment. I'm going to write to..." I peer at the signature at the bottom of the flier, "...William Fletcher and let him know we're not going anywhere, and he can put his swanky new apartment block somewhere else."

"Good," says Janie, slinging Bessie over her shoulder. The cat scrambles over the back of her neck and stretches out like a living neck warmer.

"Just because this William Fletcher is some kind of big wig developer doesn't mean he can do what he likes in this town."

"Get out," squawks Rufus.

"Exactly." I wiggle my finger at the parrot, and he grabs hold of it with his beak.

"Ow." Pain shoots through my finger and I pull it away from Rufus.

"Fuck you!" squawks the parrot.

Janie shakes her head, as much as she can with a cat wrapped around her neck and indicates the large sign above the counter.

Don't touch the parrot. He bites.

I rub my sore finger. "Point taken. I'm going to write a letter."

2

BILLY

I ring the bell for more coffee and press the letter to my nose. There's a scent of perfume which is distinctly feminine and sweet, unlike the contents of the letter.

Dear Mr. William Fletcher,

I received a notice of intention from your company informing me of the proposed plans to build an apartment block on the corner of Main and Bridal Streets in Maple Springs.

You may be unaware of the retail businesses that operate on this corner, some of which have been in their current locations for over a hundred years and passed down through generations.

In particular, my beauty salon, while boarded up now, is due to reopen in a few months' time. This was my mother's salon and has great sentimental value to me. It is more than just a retail space; a beauty salon is a place where women from the local community gather.

I ask you to reconsider your choice of location for your new development. Otherwise you may be disappointed at the opposition from local businesses and council.

Yours sincerely,
Francesca North

P.S. Pet Corner is also well loved by the local community. You should stop in some time. Owning a pet can teach you a lot about compassion.

I turn the letter over in my hand. I sympathize with these small town business owners, I truly do. But the reality is that footfall is down in town centers, and shops are struggling to stay open.

One of the reasons I chose the corner of Main and Bridal for the sight of the development was because some of the shops there are boarded up. It's a dying town center, and I'm trying to inject life back into it.

The door opens, and the fresh smell of coffee wafts in. Suzanna puts the tray down on the side table along with a fresh bowl of fruit.

"Your 2p.m. appointment's here, sir."

I stand up and move to the window. One of the landscapers is trimming the topiary trees, and I watch the green trimmings fall to the ground as he carefully shapes them.

Beyond the garden are the tennis courts where I'll have a game this afternoon with a business associate before dinner, and further beyond that, the stables.

My gaze shifts beyond my grounds to the mountains in the distance. Maple Springs is about an hour west of here, close to those mountains.

I've spent hours staring at those dark gray mountains that tower over us all. Some days the desire overcomes me to walk out of here, out of this well-ordered life, up into those mountains and never come back.

It's a stupid thought. I've built all this up myself with my own hard work and business sense. But sometimes I envy the simple lives of people like this Francesca North. She's got something to fight for, something that means something to her. I have my business and my estate, but I'd leave it all behind in a heartbeat. I don't own anything I'd fight for.

I turn back to Suzanna, who's waiting patiently by my desk. "I need you to dictate a letter."

"Certainly, sir." She pulls out her chair and sits primly on the edge, her fingers already poised over her laptop.

"Dear Francesca North,"

I glance out to the mountains again and experience a tug in my guts, a feeling I can't explain. I must be staring for a while, because Suzanna coughs delicately.

"Would you like to continue later? Your 2.p.m. is waiting in the outer office."

I shake my head. "No. Let's do this now."

I stride back to my desk and pick up the letter. The perfume scent floats off the page, and for a moment I think of the mountains.

Then I crush the letter in my fist and start dictating.

3

FRANKIE

"**C**an you believe this guy?" I wave the letter around the room. "Thinks he can buy us off by doubling the offer."

I glare around the room and Marion, the owner of Book Nook, looks down awkwardly.

"It's a very good offer," she mumbles.

I scowl at her. "Anyone else thinking of accepting this?"

Hank, the owner of the local stationery shop, shakes his head. "I'm with you Frankie. My daddy owned that store, and my daddy's daddy before him. They'll have to forcibly remove me from the place."

"Good."

I spent the evening on the group chat with the local businesswoman's network. I don't know what I'd do without that group of women. The suggestions varied from sending a letter laced with arsenic - Lizzie, to bake him homemade cookies to penetrate his dark heart - Layla.

After much outraged discussion, I settled on forming a committee to fight the development. All the girls from the network joined, even the ones who aren't currently living in

Maple Springs. Adalee, who I grew up next door to and is now a model in Seattle, offered to use her social network of thousands of followers to spread the word. But the people I most need to get on board are the affected businesses.

Which is why we're crammed into the back room of Pet Corner discussing the latest from Mr. William Fletcher. When I think about the contents of his letter, my insides twist into an angry knot.

Dear Ms. Francesca North,

I am sorry to hear that my plans inconvenience you. It often happens when progress comes to a small town.

I'm sure in its day the retail shops on the corner of Main and Bridal Streets were a thriving hub of the community. From what I've seen, that no longer seems to be the case.

In a recent visit to survey the area, I counted several vacant shops and a distinct lack of shoppers.

I hope you may find an alternate location for your salon. As it's not yet open, I don't believe it's on the plans for council repositioning.

As a mark of my generosity, I'd like to offer double the amount in relocation fees as I had on my first proposal. I hope this helps the remaining businesses have a satisfying relocation.

Yours Sincerely,

William Fletcher

P.S. Thank you for your advice about owning a pet. I do, in fact, have two Great Danes, three Alsatians, although they're more guard dogs than pets, a large tank of tropical fish, and two horses.

· · ·

The audacity of the man, thinking he can buy us off. As if we'd abandon the stores our families have owned for generations just for a bit of cash. And the way he can't help but show off his wealth in the P.S.

I put my hand on my hips and survey the room.

There are six of us whose shops will be affected by the buyout. Technically, my salon hasn't reopened yet, but considering I only signed the new lease three weeks ago, I'm angry at the landlord for taking my deposit. He must have known this was on the cards, but when I asked him about it, he pleaded ignorance.

"I don't see what else we can do," says Marion. "You can't fight a man like that who's so obviously entitled." She sniffs disdainfully.

"We'll be no match for his lawyers," says Janie. She's got Rufus on her shoulder and Bessie on her knee, who's eyeing the parrot warily. "And he's probably got the council in his pocket."

"Asshole!" squawks Rufus.

I cross my arms. "I'm not giving up. There's a council meeting next week to discuss the development. I think we should all go."

"And do what?" says Marion, shrugging her shoulders. "It won't do any good."

I glare at her. "We'll make them listen to us. Give them all the reasons why this is a bad idea. I'm happy to present our case, but I'll need your help."

"Just tell me what you need, honey," says Hank.

I grab a stack of photocopies from my bag. "I've put a petition together. Keep one of these on your front counter and get every customer to sign."

"I only have the same handful of customers who come in each week," says Marion mournfully. "So it won't be many from me."

"Marion's right," says Hank. "I don't want to give up the shop, but the truth is we don't have a lot of customers anymore."

"Then go to the other shops in town, go door to door where you live. See how much support we can get from the local community." I hand out the petition forms. "I need them back by Tuesday, along with anything specific you want me to speak about."

"I could get paw prints on the petition," says Janie. "From all the animals in the town who have come from Pet Corner."

I study her face but can't tell if she's joking or not. "Maybe not on the signature form," I say, deciding she's probably serious, "but definitely get their owners to sign."

"Okay, sure."

Everyone piles out of the back room, and I smile to myself. Mr. William Fletcher isn't going to get the better of me.

4

BILLY

Dear Mr. William Fletcher,

Thank you for your generous offer, but I regretfully decline. There are some things money can't buy, and tradition and community are two of them.

We will be fighting your planning application, and I will be presenting the council with many reasons against your plans.

Respectfully yours,

Miss Francesca North

P.S. You should try owning a pet that isn't a status symbol. There's a hamster in Pet Corner that's looking for a home.

I can't help smiling as I re-read the letter. The scent of perfume wafts off the page, and I try to imagine the woman who wears it. She's beautiful, of that I have no doubt. She's headstrong, brave, and has a sense of humor.

Too bad about the business. I hope she manages to find a location for her salon.

I put my feet up on my desk and stare out at the mountains. I wonder what she's doing now, this Miss Francesca North. Baking a fresh batch of scones? Laughing with friends over coffee? Or has she got some burly mountain man of a husband and six kids clinging to her skirts?

My stomach tightens at the thought. I pick up the letter again and breathe in the scent. No one with six kids has time for perfume.

My guess is that she's a homely small-town girl who likes to paint her friend's nails and bake chocolate cookies.

5

FRANKIE

"For god's sake, Marion," I screech. "You took the money?"

"Keep your voice down," she whispers loudly, as if afraid I might disturb her customers even though we're the only two people in the shop.

"But we're meant to be fighting this together. You're part of MABSTAD. Main and Bridal Store Owners Against Development." I pull the MABSTAD rosettes out of my bag and thrust one in her face. "I made you a badge and some banners to put up."

"I'm sorry Frankie, but you'll have to carry on without me."

"How can we carry on? Once one person goes over to the dark side, others will follow." My eyes narrow. "Who else have you told?"

Her eyes flick away nervously.

"Oh Marion." I lift my arms up in despair. "How are we meant to fight this thing if we don't stand together?"

"I'm sorry Frankie but look around. Business isn't exactly booming."

I reluctantly look around the shop. When I was a kid, this place used to be bustling.

Customers browsing the bookshelves, story time in the kids' corner, and a younger Marion bustling about making hot drinks and giving out book recommendations.

"The truth is that I was going to pack it in any way. My profits have been falling. I can't compete with the big online stores and I don't have the energy to try something new. Not like your friend Layla on the other side of town with her reading cafe. This offer is too good for me to refuse."

"But this store... you can't just let it go."

Suddenly I'm blinking back tears, remembering coming here after school with Mom. Reading Harry Potter while she gossiped with Marion. Or sometimes when Mom had clients in the salon, I'd sneak into Marion's shop and she'd bring me hot chocolate while I devoured every book on her shelves.

She puts a bony hand over mine, and the warmth is reassuring.

"Your mom would be proud of you. You remind me of her. She wouldn't have taken this lying down either. She was a fighter, even at the end," she adds quietly.

Now the tears are falling, and Marion hands me a tissue. "I don't believe we can beat this guy, Frankie. I know you want to reopen your momma's salon, but you can't bring back the past. I wish we could, but we can't. Maybe there's another way you can honor her memory."

I dab at my eyes. "She loved that salon; she loved her clients. She taught me everything she knew believing that I'd take over the business one day. I've been sweeping up hair and washing hands ever since I could walk. It's what I want to do, not just for her, but for me."

Marion nods thoughtfully and gives a big sigh. "If it really means that much to you..." She holds her hands out. "You'd better give me one of those rosettes."

"You mean you're back in MABSTAD?"

She smiles ruefully. "I'll do it for you."

"Thanks Marion." I lean over the counter and give her a hug. "We may not be able to beat this Mr. William Fletcher, but the least we can do is make it difficult for him."

I leave the store smiling and continue down the street handing out banners and rosettes at the stores. When I get home, there's another letter waiting for me.

My heart races when I see the postscript. I imagine Mr. William Fletcher is an arrogant, entitled corporate businessman with no soul. But there's a subtle irony to his letters which is intriguing.

The paper is heavy, expensive. As usual, it's typed apart from the signature at the end. It's a big signature with a flourish over the F on Fletcher. He's used a fountain pen that probably costs more than my car.

Dear Miss Francesca North,

I'm disappointed you do not find my offer acceptable. You're right. Money cannot buy everything, although you'll be amazed at how often it can buy people.

I admire your principles, but I regret I cannot change my position.

I look forward to meeting you at the council meeting on Thursday.

Yours,

William Fletcher.

P.S. Thank you for the hot tip about the hamster. I stopped by Pet Corner. What a charming store. I especially liked the eccentric store owner and her rather vocal parrot.

I'm now the proud owner of a hamster, which I've named

Rupert in honor of an English relative. You're right. There is something nice about owning a pet purely for joy.

I smile at the thought of the prim and proper Mr. William Fletcher off being told to fuck off by a parrot. I wish I could have been there to see his face.

I'm annoyed he called Janie eccentric, even though that's what Maple Springs calls her, but she's our eccentric. No outsider can make that claim on her. Just because she loves animals more than people and probably had Rufus on her shoulder, which does give the impression of a slightly unhinged pirate.

In indignation, I pull out my writing pad.

6

BILLY

DEAR MR. WILLIAM FLETCHER,

I will be representing Main and Bridal Store Owners Against Development (MABSTAD) at the council meeting on Thursday. I must warn you; we have the support of the local community.
Yours Sincerely,
Francesca North

P.S. It is the individualism of the people that makes Maple Springs the unique town that it is. You should try spending some time here and getting to know the people. You will find they're not "eccentric" but merely people who live life on their own terms and are not tied to the corporate world of conformity, as I presume you are.
P.P.S. I hope Rupert is settling in.

I read the letter again, chuckling to myself. I'm eager to meet the acerbic Francesca North.

It's an hour before the council meeting. I arrived in town early to get something to eat at a local cafe.

The council buildings are at the other end of town from where the development is taking place, and this place is bustling.

I've been sitting in Candy's Café for the last hour watching people come in and out, chat with the owners and greet each other in that familiar way you only get in small towns.

The woman who served me had blue hair in two tight bunches over her head and was wearing glitter make up. Maybe everyone here is a little eccentric, which gives it a certain charm.

I've had boards printed of the architectural plans and artists' impressions of the development. Suzanna is setting them up for me at the town hall. It'll impress the council and give my plans an inevitability; it's already planned out, and there's no turning back.

I fold the letter and place it in my laptop bag. One of my papers falls out, and I bend down to pick it up. As I stand up, I don't notice the woman coming towards me until my head crashes into her, spilling her drink onto the floor.

"I'm so sorry." We both speak at once.

I grab a handful of napkins from the counter, and we both dab at the coffee on the floor, talking over the top of each other.

"My apologies, I didn't see you."

"No, it was my fault. I was in a daze."

Our eyes meet, and I catch my breath. She's beautiful. Her eyes are deep green like the mountain forests, and her lips are plump and shiny with gloss. Red hair tumbles over her shoulders, trailing down to the soft mounds of her breasts peeking out from the top of her blouse.

But it's the scent that gets me. I'd recognize that scent anywhere. The sweet perfume of Francesca North.

There's a tug in my loins, and blood rushes to my dick. I

stand up quickly, wondering if she knows who I am and if she can tell the effect she's having on me.

She picks up the damp napkins, and I offer my hand to help her up.

"Thank you." She puts her hand in mine and gets to her feet. She's warm and soft, and I don't want to let her go.

"Let me get you another coffee."

She shakes her head. "It's fine. Thank you."

"No, I insist. I made you spill yours. What are you having?"

"It's a hot chocolate." She bites her lower lip. "With marshmallows."

I raise an eyebrow at this beautiful woman and her sugary beverage.

"Candy's does the best hot chocolates in town." She smiles, and her whole face lights up. My chest contracts and I can't take my eyes off her.

She's mine.

The words come into my head and once I've had the thought, I know it to be true.

"I'm Frankie, by the way."

She obviously hasn't figured out who I am, and when she does, she won't be smiling at me like that. This may be the only chance I get to speak to her. To convince her she's mine.

"I'm Billy." It's not a lie. I used to go by Billy when I was a kid, until I grew out of it and into William.

"What brings you to town, Billy?" she asks as we line up at the counter to get her drink. "Because I know you're not from around here."

"I have business in town," I say vaguely. "How about you? You live here?"

"My whole life, apart from a few years in Seattle."

I can't imagine this bright vivacious, friendly woman in a big city. "City life didn't suit you?"

"I missed the mountains too much. And my mom."

There's a sadness when she says it and I store that away to ask her about later.

We get to the counter and order her hot chocolate from the woman with the bright blue hair who seems to know Frankie.

As they talk, I observe her. There's no wedding ring on her finger, no burly mountain man, and no babies hanging off her skirts.

"You're not going to try one?" Frankie asks.

I shake my head. "It looks delicious, but I have to go. My assistant's waiting for me."

"Thank you for the drink."

But I can't make myself move. Once we go into that meeting she'll realize who I am and not want anything to do with me. I have to get something from her now.

"Would you have dinner with me tonight?"

Her eyes go wide in surprise. "But I don't even know you."

I shrug. "You're a beautiful woman. I'd like to take you out to dinner. That's how dating works."

"Thank you." She puts one hand on her hip and eyes me warily. I love the way she accepts the compliment with no shame. She's bold and I like that. Whatever she's searching for, she must find it because she gives a little shrug. "Yeah, why not. I'll have dinner with you."

"What's the best place in town?"

"Buffalo Bills is good. Better than the name sounds. My friend runs it and they do the best ribs."

I pull my phone out to find the place. "I'll make a reservation for eight."

She eyes me warily, no doubt wondering why she's agreed to have dinner with a stranger and if she'll actually go.

"Tell me Frankie, are you a woman of your word?"

She frowns at me. "What do you mean?"

My gaze dart to her lips, so damn plump and kissable, and I struggle to pull it back to her eyes. "Whatever happens will you be there at eight?"

She shrugs. "Of course. I said I would."

I put my little finger out in a gesture I haven't done since the schoolyard, but there's something about this woman that makes me remember simpler times.

"Pinky promise?"

Her eyes widen in surprise and she looks at my pinky and chuckles.

"Pinkie promise." Her pinkie wraps around mine and sparks of heat jump up my arm. Her eyes meet mine and the laughter turns serious. She felt that too.

"I'm going to hold you to that."

She looks confused and is probably wondering why she's agreed to dinner with a weirdo. Her hand drops suddenly out of mine. "I have to go."

Frankie slings her purse over her shoulder and walks out of the cafe.

"I'll see you at eight." I call after her. "Or before," I mutter to myself.

I've secured a date with Miss Francesca, Frankie, North. And I'm more excited about that than about the planning meeting with the council.

7

FRANKIE

I leave the cafe in a happy daze. The hottest man I've ever seen just asked me out on a date! And he was hot with a capital H! Tall and imposing with cropped dark hair and a firm jaw.

His suit was immaculate, but I saw the telltale ink creeping out from under his cuffs, suggesting that there's a dark side behind the pressed trousers and crisp shirt.

The hot chocolate tastes all the sweeter for the fact that he bought it for me. I savor every mouthful and try to bring my thoughts back to the council meeting.

It's a half hour later when I head over to the town hall. It's already busy with local residents filling the chairs. I wave to Layla and Stella and a couple of the other women from the businesswoman's network. As always, I'm thankful for their support.

My phone pings with a text and it's from Adalee wishing me luck. She's on a swimwear shoot this week, which always sounds glamorous until you speak to her and realize how dull the life of a model is with lots of downtime and creepy men hitting on her. Adalee has a strict no dating policy which has earned her the nickname of the Viking Ice Queen.

I pocket my phone and glance around the hall. There's a stage which the council members are sitting on and around the edges of the hall, easels with boards showing plans and artists' impressions.

Janie waves at me, and I take a seat next to her in the second row. Something moves in her purse and Bessie's head pops out. "You brought your cat?"

"Shhh, she looks around furtively while pushing the furry head into her purse. "Bessie likes to know what's going on."

I don't say anything about what might happen if Bessie gets loose or needs the loo. I should be thankful she didn't bring Rufus.

"Are you nervous?" Janie asks.

I take my cue cards out of my bag. "A little, but I've practiced so many times. I nearly know it by heart."

"You'll be great." She squeezes my arm encouragingly.

"So which one's Mr. William Fletcher?" I say as I scan the room.

"I think it's him." She points to a cluster of chairs next to the stage. I start in surprise. It's the man from the cafe, and he's starting straight at me.

"Oh no." My heart sinks as realization dawns. The hottest man I've ever met is Mr. William Fletcher. "He said his name was Billy."

I fill Janie in on my cafe encounter and she bristles at the story.

"What a jerk, trying to buy you a hot chocolate to butter you up. He probably bumped into you on purpose."

I glance at 'Billy' and he's still looking at me. His gaze in intense and heat floods my cheeks. "I don't think he did."

"I wouldn't put anything past a guy like him."

"He came across as quite nice."

Janie turns in her seat and gives me a hard stare. "You like him."

"No I don't." Heat spreads up my neck. Because she's right. I'm suddenly defending him.

Janie laughs. "Oh yes, you do."

"I most definitely do not. He's trying to take Mom's salon. How could I be interested in him?"

"Hmmm." Janie just nods and smiles. Bessie mewls as if in agreement.

I'm saved from further argument by a councilor clearing her throat.

The meeting begins with Mr. William Fletcher presenting his plans. He's confident and charming, and I'm finding it hard to take in anything he says because I'm enjoying just watching him.

There are questions from the audience, and he handles them with ease. Janie nudges me. "Aren't you going to say anything?"

I give her a dirty look. "Of course. I was just about to." But I'm suddenly nervous about speaking to Mr. Fletcher. I raise my hand, and his eyes are instantly on me.

"Miss North, isn't it?" Damn, he must have known who I was in the cafe. Maybe he did run into me on purpose.

"You're proposing to get rid of the shops on the corner, but some of those have been there for a hundred years." I gain confidence as I speak and my voice gets stronger. "We are a community here in Maple Springs, and a community needs its heart. You're proposing that people come to live in apartments without a beating heart."

There are murmurs of approval from around the room.

He looks at me intently for a moment. "You make a good point, Miss North, and I believe we'll be hearing from you in just a moment. But in answer to your question, there are many other shops in the area that are prospering and will adequately provide the, as you call it, beating heart of the community."

I sit down again, feeling annoyed. This man has no heart, so how can he know about the heart of a community?

There are a few more questions, and then it's my turn.

I walk to the podium clasping my cue cards. Mr. William Fletcher, or should I say Billy, is watching me attentively, looking quite smug.

"I'm representing MABSTAD, Main and Bridal Store Owners Against Development."

I survey a sea of expectant faces, but I can't help being drawn to him. His intense eyes are focused on me, and he's smiling slightly. My stomach does a little flip. Damn, he's hot. I open my mouth to speak, but no words come out. All I can think about is how much I'd like to kiss that smug smile off his face.

I lick my lips nervously and glance down at my cue cards. I can get through this if I don't look at him again. I look up and focus on Janie and the little furry head poking out from her oversized purse.

"Progress can take many forms, and new development at the expense of history and tradition is not the only way to move forward."

I warm to my speech as I go on, and at the end of it the local residents give me a standing ovation. I chance a glance at Mr. William Fletcher and he's clapping slowly, a wary look on his face. I grin widely, hoping I've got him rattled.

I answer a few questions from the councilors and the crowd and then take my seat next to Janie. "You were brilliant."

"Well done, honey." Hank leans over from his seat behind us and claps me on the shoulder. "That'll show them."

The meeting ends, and I'm leaving with Janie when there's a tap on my shoulder. I turn around to find a smug

Mr. Fletcher and am annoyed when my stomach does a little flip.

"We have a dinner date."

"I don't think so," I say, spinning around. "I don't dine with the devil."

He looks amused. "You told me you were a woman of your word. And we made…" he waggles his little finger, "…a pinky promise."

I stare at his finger as annoyance blooms in my chest. I can't believe he's going to hold me to this.

"That was before I knew who you were."

"Am I really that terrible?"

"Yes." I fold my arms across my chest. "Yes, you are."

"Then tell me all about it over dinner. Tell me all about this town and why you're fighting so hard."

I eye him skeptically.

"You never know, you might change my mind."

I scoff. "Don't pretend you're going to back down. Guys like you don't back down."

His eyes go dark and something flashes across his face. Is that jealousy? But that would be absurd. "What do you know about guys like me?"

"I know you'll do anything it takes to get your development through, and you don't care who you hurt along the way."

His eyes flash dangerously. "Is that what you think of me, Francesca?"

I open my mouth to speak, but words don't come out. He's so close I can smell his expensive aftershave and a horsey scent and something deep and musky that's all him.

His gaze rakes over my body and heat flares up inside me. There's an ache deep in my core and my nipple harden into peaks.

"I'd like to find out more about you," he says softly, "and if you'd like to find out who I really am, I'll see you at Buffalo Bills at eight."

He walks out of the hall, his perfect ass tight in his immaculate suit. I watch him go, my mind in a whirl, my body overheating and my panties on fire.

8

BILLY

It's five minutes to eight, and I'm seated at Buffalo Bills watching the door. My fingers drum the table, and as the minutes tick by I become more impatient.

At five minutes past eight, she walks in the door. I let out a breath I didn't know I was holding. Francesca looks stunning. Her hair is tied back off her face, the fiery color offset against a green summer dress that hugs her curves.

She sees me and nods, her face set in a serious frown. I'll make it my mission to make her smile tonight. To make her laugh.

She takes a seat in the booth opposite me.

"I'm glad you came."

She eyes me warily. "I thought it was only fair to give you a chance."

I pass her a menu hoping it will relax her. "What's good here?"

"They do the best ribs in town."

"Ribs it is then."

We place our orders, and I study her over the table. She's

studying me back, a determined set to her face. I long to get to know her, to find out what drives that determination.

"What I don't understand is that you haven't even opened your beauty salon yet. Why not take up the relocation offer and open it on Burlap Street?"

She arranges her cutlery on the table and speaks slowly as if explaining it to a child.

"Firstly, Burlap Street is at the wrong end of town. No one goes there. Secondly…" she takes a deep breath and straightens the folk. "I want to stay in the place where my mom had her salon."

It's sentimental reasons, it's always sentimental reasons why people don't want to relocate as if the building holds the memories and not the heart.

The waiter brings our drinks and I take a tentative sip of my beer. It's from Bear's Brewery, a local brewery up in the mountain's and is surprisingly good. I make a mental note to have Suzanna order me a few crates.

"Why did your mom close it down?"

She looks at me for a long time and just when I think she's not going to answer she looks down and her voice is barely a whisper. "She passed away last year."

Oh shit. No wonder it means so much to her. And I'm the big asshole who's taking that away from her. "I'm so sorry. I didn't know."

She waves her hand dismissively. "Why would you? Mom opened that salon when I was a baby. She was incredibly proud of it, going into business while raising a family. I spent a lot of my childhood there. It's where I grew up, darting in and out of the shops along those streets."

"It has great sentimental value to you."

She looks at me sharply. "Not just for me. It's where people used to meet."

The ribs arrive, and she keeps talking.

"That salon was bustling on a Saturday, all the women of Maple Springs getting their hair or nails done. You'd hear all the gossip, but not just the malicious stuff--who was struggling, who needed help with the kids, who needed a safe place to stay for a few nights. Mom would spend Saturday in the salon, but after it closed up, she'd go around delivering care packages or collecting children for the night to give someone a break."

"She sounds like an amazing woman."

"She was." Francesca picks at her ribs. "Mom died of breast cancer. She worked until she was too sick to work anymore. I shut the place down while I cared for her. I promised her before she died that I'd reopen the salon. Because it's not just about doing hair and nails. It really is about community."

She blinks back tears, and I pull out my handkerchief and hand it over.

Francesca smiles thinly as she takes it. "I don't know anybody who still carries a handkerchief. Does it have your initials?"

I hold my hands up. "Monogrammed in the corner."

She laughs, and the sprinkling of freckles across her nose dance as she smiles.

She wipes her eyes and takes a drink. "How about you then? Prove that I'm wrong about you."

I take a mouthful of ribs and chew slowly, wondering where to start. "These are delicious by the way."

"Stop stalling." She pokes a rib at me and damn I wish this was a proper date and not something I coerced her into. "Tell me the worst."

"I grew up in a large estate on the edge of Portland. My father was an investor and I dutifully followed him, going to business school and getting into property development."

I take another bite of rib to stop myself from talking. It's a privileged and boring life and I don't want to bore her with it.

"That's it? That's your life story?"

"Sadly yes. I have several business interests and I'm always looking for opportunities to get small towns thriving again."

She frowns. "How is this meant to get Maple Springs thriving?"

"People have moved further and further away from the centers of towns. They live in big houses spread out in the suburbs. They drive more and see their neighbors less. By building residential areas in the centers of towns, it brings residents back into the heart of the community. Gets them spending locally and boosts the local economy."

She stares at me thoughtfully hopefully realizing that I'm not the heartless asshole she thinks I am.

"So you see, Francesca, we're not too dissimilar with what we want. It's just unfortunate in this case that you have sentimental attachment to the space."

She bristles, and I know I've said the wrong thing. "It's more than my sentimental attachment. The whole town loves those shops."

"Then why are so many of them going out of business?" I say gently.

"Can I get you any dessert?" the waitress asks, making us both start.

"No." Francesca says quickly.

I order the bill and turn the conversation back to safer ground. But her guards are up. I've fucked this up and I hope like hell I get another chance to speak to her.

As she talks about the shops and the people of the town, I watch her lips move unable to take my gaze from them even as I know there's no way in hell she's letting me kiss her tonight.

By the time I walk her to her car, I'm beginning to feel a very uncomfortable feeling about Miss Francesca North, one that starts in my dick and tugs at me all the way to my heart.

It's three days later when I get the phone call. They've ruled in my favor; the development is going ahead.

I should feel elated. I should be celebrating. But all I can think about is how devastated Francesca will be.

9

FRANKIE

"Where do you want the lizard feed?"

Janie scans the open boxes spread out across the floor of her back room. "Put it with the reptile bits in the corner."

I place it in the box next to a stack of fake rocks and hides. "When is your moving date?"

"I don't know yet. I've not heard anything from the council."

"They're probably too busy salivating over the big payouts they're getting from the new development."

The bell from the shop jangles, letting us know a customer has come in the door.

"Fuck off," squawks Rufus, but even he sounds more deflated than usual.

Janie goes through to the shop while I start on the next shelf. I'm sorting fish tank ornaments when she comes back, followed by Bessie mewling mournfully.

"Someone here to see you." She scoops up Bessie and slings the cat over her shoulder.

"Who?"

She gives me a dark look that I can't interpret. "Go see for yourself."

I go through to the shop and find Mr. William Fletcher in an immaculate suit and not a hair out of place, bent over with his finger wiggling in the hamster cage.

"Be careful they don't bite it off."

He pulls his finger back quickly. "I'm thinking of getting a friend for Rupert. He seems lonely."

I don't know why he's here. If it's to gloat I don't want to hear it. I just wish he didn't look so damn hot.

"Congratulations," I say, folding my arms across my chest. "You won."

"Francesca..."

Whenever he says my full name in his rumbling low voice it sets heat waves from my lower belly down my legs and makes me want to jump his well suited bones.

"Can you just call me Frankie? Everyone does."

"If you call me Billy."

The name doesn't suit him and an arch an eyebrow. "Is that what everyone calls you?"

He chuckles. "No one's called me Billy since I was twelve. But I like it coming from you."

He takes a step closer and my breath catches. No man has a right to be this good looking, especially asshole developers. "What do you want, Billy? Did you come to gloat?"

His face goes serious. "Of course not."

I believe him. He was genuine over dinner. I believe he has good motives that aren't all money driven. But I can't forgive him for what he's about to do to my mom's salon.

"I was really touched when you told me about your mom. I wanted to do something, so I've donated a hundred thousand dollars to breast cancer research."

My mouth drops open. "That's a lot of money."

He waves his hand in the air. "It's nothing. If it means people like your mom don't have to suffer, then it's worth it."

Tears threaten my eyes and I look away before he can see. Damn this asshole for being good looking and generous.

"Thank you. That's very generous."

He smiles, and the affect is devastating. My core clenches tight and damp head floods my panties.

"Will you have dinner with me tonight?"

My mouth drops open and indignation floors me. He's still trying to buy me off. "Are you trying to buy me?"

"No..." he holds up his hands and takes another step toward me. But I'm not falling for his charms, no matter how much my body wants to.

"Is money your answer for everything?"

"That's not what I meant, Frances... Frankie." His face looks stricken, he mustn't be used to not being able to buy people.

I swallow down my anger straighten my shoulders and channel the inner strength momma instilled in me. "I appreciate the donation, Mr. Fletcher. It's a very thoughtful thing to do, but it doesn't change the fact of how I feel about you."

He takes a step forward, and he's so close I can smell his expensive cologne and heady scent. "And how do you feel about me?"

His eyes bore into mine and my equilibrium wavers. He's got rough stubble on his chin and I wonder what that stubble would feel like grazing my thighs.

"Because I like you, a lot."

His lips crash into mine, and they're warm and firm, and they set off a shiver that runs all the way between my legs. And before I know it, I'm kissing him back. My lips are pulling at his, and my tongue darts into his mouth. His arm slides around my waist, and it feels so damn good to be held by him.

Then I remember Mom and her shop and who he is. I pull away, wiping my tingling lips. I'm disgusted at myself and aroused, and there's a place inside me that just wants to keep kissing him.

I back away shaking my head. "No. You don't get to destroy my dreams and then kiss me like that."

"But Frankie..."

"No." I cut him off. "I'm grateful that you donated the money, but it doesn't change things between us. You'll always be the man who destroyed Mom's salon, and I won't ever feel any differently towards you. There are some things money can't buy, Mr. William Fletcher."

I brush past him fighting back tears and push my way onto the street. My heart's racing and my mind's in a whirl, and my treacherous body is screaming at me to go back and get that man's hands on me again.

Behind me Rufus squawks "Asshole." And I repeat the word over and over in my head as I run to my car and drive home with tears streaming down my face.

10

BILLY

*I*t's an hour later when I pull up outside Frankie's place. I had to plead with the eccentric pet shop owner to give me the address. When she heard my reasons she started to soften up, and after I bought two more hamsters, she finally handed it over.

I grab my rolled up planning sketches from the trunk and tuck the shoe box with the hamsters in it under one arm.

"Wish me luck, guys," I say to the hamsters as I knock on the door.

After a few moments Frankie opens the door, and when she sees me she starts to shut it again.

"Let me explain, Frankie." I wedge my boot in the door, and she frowns at my foot, but I'm not budging. "You need to see the new plans."

She pushes the door against my foot scowling when it doesn't move. "Why would I want to see those?"

"Because I changed them for you."

She stops trying to crush my foot and squints at me suspiciously. "What do you mean?"

38

"Let me show you."

She looks at me hard for a moment and I know I should be thinking about making it up to her, but all I can think about is what those pouty lips would feel like wrapped around my cock. This woman's had me in a spin ever since her perfume wafted out of the first letter.

"You've got five minutes." She opens the door, and I follow her into the house.

I put my plans and my box down on the dining room table. There's a scrabbling noise coming from the shoe box, and she looks at me quizzically.

"I bought two more hamsters, Gerald and Ralph."

She raises an eyebrow. "More English relatives?"

"My brothers."

A smile plays on her lips, and I relax a little. Although now she looks so damn adorable, half pissed off and half forgiving, that my dick stirs to life.

I spread the plans out on the table, pushing the hamsters to the side and trying to focus. "After our meeting I revised the plans."

She's got her arms folded and her hair trails down her shoulders, the ends of it tickling the tops of her breasts making it hard to focus.

I point to the ground floor of the plan. She leans in to see what I'm showing her. And God help me, I can see right down the crease of her cleavage to the soft white domes of flesh.

"I don't get it." She straightens up and so does my dick.

"I've kept the retail block on the ground floor."

She leans in again, and I can't look at her or I'm going to do something indecent.

"Look here." I point to the names written above the shops.

"Pet Corner..." she reads. "Frankie's beauty salon."

She looks at me and realization spreads across her face. "The shops are staying?"

"Yes. That's what I was trying to tell you today. The ground floor will be retail, so the shops that are there now can stay if they want to."

"But what about your apartments?"

"They'll still be there; we'll just have seven floors instead of eight."

She considers this nibbling on the end of her finger. "That's fewer apartments. Won't you lose money?"

I shrug like it's no big deal, because it isn't. "It's not as financially attractive as eight levels. There are six fewer apartments we could have put in the block. But as someone wise once told me, there are more important things than money."

A grin spread across Frankie's face. "I get to keep Mom's salon?"

"Yes, you all get to stay. I'd like to renovate the spaces, give the shops a face lift in keeping with the new apartments. With residents living above it could again be the hub of Maple Springs."

She throws her arms around me excitedly, pushing the wind out of me. "Thank you, thank you!"

She pulls back and looks at the plans again. "But why would you do that?"

I take her hand and turn her around so she's looking at me. "Because from the moment I read that first prissy letter and smelled your perfume wafting off it, I knew you were the woman for me."

She bristles. "It was not prissy."

I raise my eyebrows. "Uh-huh, Miss Francesca North."

She laughs and I'm so glad to see the laughter in her eyes. "Then when I ran into you at the cafe, you were as beautiful as I imagined. You're bold and determined and kind and I knew from that moment you were mine. When I realized what that space meant to you, I knew I had to do whatever it took to help you keep it. Your dreams are my dreams now Frankie."

She sighs against me and I tilt her chin up to look at me. "So you can stop pretending I don't affect you because I know I do."

She shrugs, and there's a mischievous look in her eye. "You're okay."

"Okay? Come here, minx."

I pull her towards me and capture her smiling mouth in a kiss. She kisses me back, her lips soft and warm and inviting. Our tongues find each other, entwining as the kiss deepens.

The feel of her lips and her body close to mine cause my dick to ache with need. I slide my hand down her body and around her waist, pressing her toward me so she can feel my hardness.

She moans softly in my mouth, the sweetest sound, which sends a shock of blood to my cock. I move my lips down her throat, savoring the soft skin. Her perfume fills my senses and drives me wild with want.

She lets out another moan as I brush her earlobe with my lips.

"How do you like me now, Frankie?" I whisper into her ear, letting my breath tickle her delicate skin.

"I like you more and more by the minute." She giggles and the sound make my body heat for her.

My hand slides under her skirt, and her skin is on fire under my touch. I coast over her thighs until my fingertips skim her panties. The roughness of the lace fabric combined with the heat and dampness causes my cock to throb. Every new discovery of this woman is driving me wild.

I run my hand over the damp gusset of her panties. "And how about now? How do you like it now?"

"I like it," she moans. Her head tilts back, and her eyes close in ecstasy.

"What do you like?" my voice comes out as a rasp but I want to hear her say it.

"I like you touching me, Billy."

My fingers strum her through the panties while my mouth moves down to the tops of her breasts. She shudders under my touch and her breathing turns to needy pants.

"Tell me what you like."

"I like your fingers on my panties." Her words come out in breathy gasps that make my cock ache.

"Go on."

"It feels good," she moans. "You're making my pussy wet."

The dirty talk is almost too much. I want to get my cock out and thrust it into her sweet pussy, but I make myself hold back. I want to take my time and make the confident Francesca North come undone on the palm of my hand.

I slide the fabric of her panties to the side, and she's dripping wet. Her sweet nectar oozes onto my fingers as I stroke her folds.

Her clitoris is slick with her juice as I tap my fingers against her sensitive button, feeling it harden under my touch.

She cries out as I glide my fingers inside. She's so warm and tight and my cock sends out a protest, wanting to be inside her.

She rides my palm and I slide deeper inside focusing on her pleasure and watching the way every movement transforms her face.

She's panting and moaning, and it's the most beautiful sound I've ever heard.

My hand collides with her pussy with every thrust as she bears down on me. I pump harder and faster until she cries out and rocks into my hand. I push into her hard and hold her there as she shudders in ecstasy.

Once Frankie stops trembling, I slowly remove my hand. Her eyes open slowly, and there's a dreamy look in her eyes.

"How do you feel about me now?" I ask.

"I think I might love you," she says with a smile.

11

FRANKIE

y body feels like it's floating, and I know I'm smiling like an idiot, but damn that was good. But I'm not satisfied, I need something more. Which is good, because the serious way Billy's looking at me and the tent in his trousers make me think more is coming. Much, much more.

Feeling like a brazen hussy, I look him in the eye as I reach under my skirt and slide my panties off.

I hold them up on one finger and raise an eyebrow at him, a smile playing on my lips.

"You want to finish this, Mr. William Fletcher?"

He takes a sharp intake of breath and snatches my panties off me. "Call me Billy."

He pushes me up against the table and with one hand clears the plans onto the floor.

The shoebox wobbles but stays on the table. "Watch out for the hamsters."

"Fuck the hamsters."

The hungry look in his eyes tugs at my core and sends a fresh surge of wetness between my legs.

He undoes his pants, and they fall to the floor. His cock stands tall and proud, and there's a purple throbbing vein from the base to the tip.

My eyes go wide, and my pussy gushes. "Oh my god."

He smiles wickedly. "You think you can handle it?"

I nod. "Oh yeah."

He grabs my ass and lifts me onto the table. "Good, because I'm going to bury myself in your pussy, Frankie."

The uptight Me. William Fletcher likes to talk dirty. His words makes me hot all over and wet with need. He pulls my skirts up, and his dick rubs against my thigh.

"And I'm not using protection. I want you for my own, and I want to bury my seed in you. Do you understand?"

A thrill runs through me at the primal words. There is way more to this man than a corporate developer. And I know suddenly and with certainty that he's the man for me, now and forever.

"I want that too."

"Say it, Frankie. Tell me what you want." His dick grazes my pussy, his tip brushing against my sensitive folds as he teases me with it.

"I want you to fuck me," I say breathlessly.

He moans at the words. "Say it again." He presses at the opening of my pussy, and I'm on fire with need.

"I want you to fuck me. I want you to put your seed in me, Billy." He moans when I say his name, and his dick slides into me.

I cry out at the pressure as he pushes forward, filling me up. He stops halfway and my pussy relaxes, adjusting to his girth.

"How does that feel?"

"Good. It feels good."

My eyes flutter closed and I enjoy the sensation of my man slowly filling me up.

I adjust around him but he's going too slow. I want more, I want deeper but he's holding back. A needy whimper escapes my lips.

"What is it? What do you want?"

"I want all of you." I moan.

"Not yet." He grits his teeth and he must be afraid he'll hurt me but I can take it. I want the pain with the pleasure.

"Please…" I don't care that I'm begging it makes it hotter. I'll beg all day for him to give me what I need.

"Please what?" His cock is sitting halfway inside me, and I'm aching to feel all of him.

"Please, Billy, fuck me all the way."

"If that's what you want." He grins wickedly and thrusts hard and sudden and my pussy is on fire. I cry out, and he slides out and thrusts again. My pussy slides up and down his shaft as he pulls me toward him.

"Billy," I moan with every thrust.

"Say my name again," he pants.

"Billy!" I cry as he slams into me. He's pounding me now, fucking me hard, and I love it. My pussy crashes into him, and suddenly I'm coming as hard and fast as a freight train.

"Billy, Billy Billy!" I scream.

"Frankie." He grabs my ass and impales me on his cock. I feel his cum shoot into me as we both cum together.

We're still panting a few minutes later when he eases himself out of me.

He lifts me off the table and smooths down my skirt. "You okay?"

I smile at him dreamily. "More than okay."

There's a scratching noise, and we both turn to the table. The lid has been knocked off the shoe box, and two anxious hamster faces are peering out.

"I didn't know we had an audience," says Billy. "I hope they enjoyed the show."

"They look a bit stunned." I grab the lid and put it over the shoe box. "No more peeking," I tell the hamsters.

Billy chuckles and I smile up at him, wondering at the magic of progress. A few weeks ago I thought I was happy as I prepared to open my salon. Now, I'm more than happy. I'm fulfilled. I have a future with a good man and potentially a family of our own and a menagerie of pets. Life is definitely progressing in the right direction.

EPILOGUE

FRANKIE

Five years later...

"Another letter for you, Frankie."

The mailman waves the envelope at me and puts it down on the front desk.

"Thanks," I call, hurrying through the salon.

I have ten minutes before my next client, so I snatch up the envelope and rip it open, breathing in the faint scent of his cologne.

"Is it a letter from Daddy?" asks our three-year-old, pulling on my skirt.

"Yes it is, sweetie."

"Can I see?" She holds her hands out, and I show her the letter, thankful she can't read yet because there's bound to be something dirty in there.

She looks at it solemnly and hands it back. "Can I go play with the kittens?"

"As long as Janie's not too busy."

I walk her out of the salon and into Pet Corner next door. Janie waves her in and Rufus squawks happily calling her an asshole. I'm not crazy about my baby girl learning how to cuss from a parrot, but hey, life is never perfect. Although it's pretty damned close.

"Send her back when you need to." I tell Janie. "I've got one more client, and then I'm done for the day."

"You should be taking it easy." She eyes my pregnant belly pointedly.

"I'm fine. Two more weeks and I'll put my feet up."

She sees the envelope I'm clutching in my hand and smiles. "A letter from Billy?"

I grin, and she rolls her eyes. "I don't know why you two write each other letters; you see each other every day. What can there possibly be to say?"

I raise my eyebrows suggestively. "You'd be surprised." I give her a cheeky grin as I duck back into my salon.

The three hairdressing stations are full of clients chatting with the hairdressers and so is the nail bar. We have two treatment rooms out the back as well.

We have loyal regular customers and offer a discount to the residents of the apartments above us.

It took a little over a year for the apartments to be built and the salon to be renovated, and we've been busy ever since. I have a fantastic team working for me and a manager who'll look after the place while I'm on maternity leave.

Billy and I were married six months after we met, and I moved into his estate while the development was happening.

Now we have the penthouse apartment right here above the salon. Billy's become a small-town man, getting involved in the community and helping to breathe new life into the main street. On the weekends we go hiking into the mountains, stopping off at Bear's Brewery when we can.

We write to each other every week. It reminds us of how we met, the formality of the letters a private joke between us.

I sink into my office chair and pull out the letter. With my feet up, I start to read.

Dear Mrs. Francesca Fletcher,

I trust this letter finds you well.

I wanted to inform you that you looked stunning in your yellow sundress yesterday. When I came into the salon to see you after work, you took my breath away. It's possible it's the glow of pregnancy, or you could just be the most beautiful woman I've ever seen.

If you hadn't had been in a room full of clients, I would have bent you over the nail bar and taken you from behind in front of the full-length mirror.

Regrettably, there were clients to think of, and so my plan wasn't acceptable at this time.

I write this as you are in the shower; your singing can be heard throughout the apartment. I have always found your voice sweet, but our daughter is covering her ears and asking me when mommy will stop wailing.

I regret I cannot be in the shower with you this morning. I'd love to cover your body with soap suds and gently wash you all over. I'd start by soaping your soft breasts, tugging on the nipples until they harden...

"Frankie, your next appointment's here."

I stand up quickly and stuff the letter in my pocket. My heart's racing, and my panties are wet.

"Coming," I call.

I take a few deep breaths and try to put the image of my husband soaping me down in the shower out of my head.

I'll finish the letter tonight in bed. I'll read it out loud to Mr. William Fletcher as he does indecent things to me.

My body thrills in anticipation of what's coming.

But first I have a salon to run.

———

GET YOUR FREE BOOK

Sign up to the Sadie King mailing list for a FREE book!

You'll be the first to hear about exclusive offers, bonus content and all the news from Sadie King.

Allie is a bonus book in the Curvy Girl Can series exclusive to my newsletter subscribers.

To claim your free book visit:
authorsadieking.com/bonus-scenes

BOOKS BY SADIE KING

Maple Springs

Small Town Sisters

Candy's Café

All the Single Dads

Men of Maple Mountain

Curvy Girls Can

The Carter Family

Wild Heart Mountain

Military Heroes

Wild Riders MC

Mountain Heroes

Biker Brothers of Winter Town

Sunset Coast

Sunset Security

Underground Crows MC

Filthy Rich Love

Men of the Sea

For a full list of titles check out the Sadie King website

www.authorsadieking.com

ABOUT THE AUTHOR

Sadie King is a USA Today Best Selling Author of short instalove romance.

She lives in New Zealand with her ex-military husband and raucous young son.

When she's not writing she loves catching waves with her son, running along the beach, and drinking good wine, preferably with a book in hand.